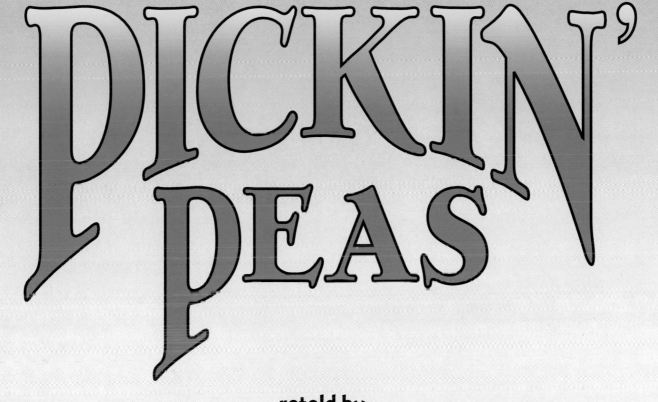

PICKIN' PEAS

retold by
Margaret Read MacDonald

pictures by
Pat Cummings

HarperCollins*Publishers*

CORE
HL

Pickin' Peas
Text copyright © 1998 by Margaret Read MacDonald
Illustrations copyright © 1998 by Pat Cummings
Manufactured in China. All rights reserved.
http://www.harperchildrens.com

Library of Congress Cataloging-in-Publication Data
MacDonald, Margaret Read, date
    Pickin' peas / retold by Margaret Read MacDonald ; pictures by Pat Cummings.
        p.   cm.
    Summary: Because a pesky rabbit picks peas from her garden, a little girl catches
it and puts it in a box, but that doesn't solve the problem.
    ISBN 0-06-027235-X.
    [1. Rabbits—Fiction.   2. Peas—Fiction.]   I. Cummings, Pat, ill. II. Title.
PZ7.M4784187Pi   1998   95-26133
[E]—dc20   CIP
                                                                              AC

4   5   6   7   8   9   10
❖

**For all the kids and rabbits
of Jennings County, Indiana
—M.R.M.**

**For Lerato
—P.C.**

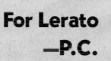

Little Girl planted a garden of peas.

She thought a minute.

"I do believe if I turn back around the end of this row, I can CATCH HIM!"

Little Girl started tiptoeing back up the row she'd already picked.

There was Mr. Rabbit hopping along down at the end of that row.

"Pickin' peas.
Land on my knees!"

Come July, those peas got ripe and ready to eat.

Little Girl went out in her garden. Started going down the row. Picking peas. Singing,

"Pickin' peas.
Put 'em in my pail."

Just picking off the biggest ones. Left the little bitty ones to grow some more.

A pesky rabbit lived down in the holler.

He jumped in the row behind her. . . . Started hopping along eating her peas. Singing,

"Pickin' peas. Land on my knees!"

Every time he'd sing, he'd give a jump. And he'd land on his knees every time.

He came down that row eating up all the peas she'd left behind.

Mr. Rabbit was moving along just one row behind Little Girl.

When she'd turn the corner at the east end of the garden and start DOWN a row, he'd turn the corner at the west end of the garden and start UP a row.

"Pickin' peas.
Put 'em in my pail."

"Pickin' peas.
Land on my knees!"

After a while Little Girl got to feeling like somebody was following her.

Said to herself, "I think I'll cut my song off right short and see what I hear.

"Pickin' peas.
Put 'em in my . . ."

Listened. Heard . . .

"Land on my knees!"

Little Girl said, "AHA! I do believe that pesky rabbit is in my garden. I do believe he's following me. I do believe he's PICKIN' MY PEAS!"

She crept up behind him real quiet.

"Pickin' peas.
Land on my knees!"

She reached out . . .

"Pickin' peas.
Land on my . . .

. . . WOAPP!"

She CAUGHT HIM.

Said, "Mr. Rabbit. What's that you were singing just now?"

Mr. Rabbit scrunched up.

Said, "Ooooooohhhh, I was singing, uhhh . . .

'Diggin' up roots.
Land on my foots. . . .'"

"That's not what you were singing!" and she squeezed him harder.

"What were you singing?"

"Oooooooooohh," he said in a little squinchy voice.

"I was singing,

'Pickin' peas.
Land on my knees!'"

"That's what I THOUGHT you were singing," said Little Girl. "You were eating up my peas, weren't you?"

". . . Mmmm, maybe."

"Well, you won't pick MY peas anymore. I'm going to take you home. Put you in a box. And keep you there till pea-picking season is OVER."

She took that rabbit home. Put him in a box. Shut the lid down real tight. Cooked a mess of peas. And ate them all up.

"Well, THAT was good."

Then Little Girl heard Mr. Rabbit hopping around inside that box. He was singing,

"Pickin' peas. Land on my knees!"

"Mr. Rabbit, what's that you're doing in there?"

"Trying to dance, but it's too crowded in here. Take me out and put me up on top of the box. I'll dance and entertain you."

"Let me see that."

She took him out and put him up on top of the box. And he began to dance and sing.

"Pickin' peas.
Land on my knees!
Heard my momma callin' me
RIGHT over there."

Every time he sang "RIGHT over there," he gave a little jump to the right.

"That's GOOD dancing!" said Little Girl.

"Put me up on that big chest by the window and I could dance even BETTER," said Mr. Rabbit.

Little Girl put him up on the big chest by the window, and Mr. Rabbit started really cutting up.

"Pickin' peas.
Land on my knees!
Heard my momma callin' me
RIGHT over there."

Little Girl was clapping and laughing. "I LOVE your dancing, Mr. Rabbit."

"Put me up on that windowsill and I could REALLY dance," said Mr. Rabbit.

So Little Girl picked him up. Set him down on that broad windowsill by the open window.

Mr. Rabbit was jumping up and down and kicking up his heels.

"Pickin' peas.
Land on my knees!"

When he got to the end, he gave one tremendous LEAP . . .

"Heard my momma callin' me
RIGHT over there."

. . . and OUT the window he went.

Mr. Rabbit ran off through the
garden calling,

"Picked your peas,
And I landed on my knees
Gonna eat all I want
'Cause you can't catch me!"

I'd like to say that's the last Little Girl saw of that rabbit. But I'm afraid he was right back there the next morning.

Pickin' peas . . .

and landin'

on his

knees!

About this tale

This story was elaborated from a tale collected in Calhoun, Alabama, and published in *Southern Workman*, Vol. 26, No. 12 (December 1897), and from a turn-of-the-century variant in "Folklore from Elizabeth City County, Virginia," *Journal of American Folklore*, Vol. 35 (1922), pp. 273–4, as told by Sarah Demings.

When telling this story, it is fun to repeat the "pickin' peas" refrain twice and let the listeners join in. I make a picking motion and slap one hand into the other palm on the word "pail." When Mr. Rabbit sings, I slap my legs on "land on my knees." My sources did not record the tellers' tunes. Use the one I invented (previous page), or invent your own.

The story is also fun to act out, dividing your listeners into "young gardeners" and "pesky rabbits." Read it, tell it, act it out . . . and have fun!